In loving Memory of Michael Anthony Smallwood Starks.

All Songs by Michael and Tennessee Ward. Published by Monkeyfeather Music (ASCAP) and Orbitsurfer (ASCAP).

Performed by the incredible Tennessee Ward and the wonderful Paulette Ely.

Mixed by the amazing Curt Schneider.

Published By

Monkeyfeather Books
PO Box 520126
Salt Lake City, Utah 84152

A special thanks to Propellerheads Reason software. Direct from Sweden!

ISBN: 978-0-9762800-9-5
Library of Congress: 2008937186
www.mikeandthebike.com

10 9 8 7 6 5 4 3 2 1

Mike and the Bike meet Lucille the Wheel

Written by **Michael Ward**

Illustrated by **Bob Thomson**

Foreword by **Lance Armstrong**

Hi everybody, this is Lance.

Welcome to another cycling adventure from the world of
Mike and the Bike.

In today's story we'll meet a very special girl.
She's quite the little mechanic,
and she may even give Mike
a run for his money on the bike!

So once again, hop on
and go for a ride as
Mike and the Bike meet Lucille the Wheel.

LANCE ARMSTRONG

Hello once again from the world of the bike,

a place that is home to a boy called Mike.

It's a world that is fueled by imagination

and a generous dose of determination.

It's these two ingredients that combine to propel you

to all of the places that enchant and compel you.

In today's tale our boy Mike will meet

a new cycling friend who lives just up the street.

Let's set off on a ride where dreams become real

as Mike and the Bike meet Lucille the Wheel.

The small town of Colberg is where we begin,
a town not unlike one where you may have been.
Colberg is located far and away
from big skyscraper buildings and traffic delay.
It's a small mountain town and the roads are so quiet
it's a bike riding heaven, one could never deny it.

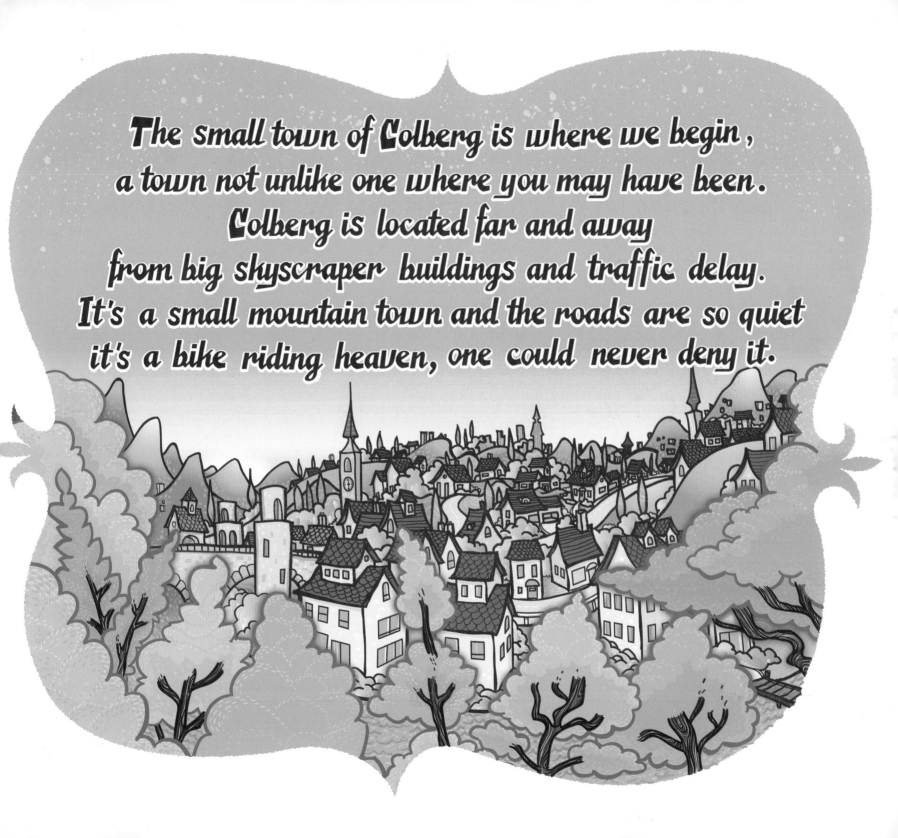

He's waited all week for his most favorite treat, the moment his bicycle tires hit the street.

The garage door is open,
there's someone inside.
Why, it seems to be a cyclist
preparing for a ride.
The garage is equipped with
all manner of wrenches
and tools and stools and
mechanic's workbenches.
As the neighbor inside
tweaks a spoke on a wheel —

She turns
to our Mike
and says,

"Hi, I'm Lucille!"

"I was just going out for a Saturday spin. Would you care to join me? I'm about to begin."

So the two pedal on down the quiet avenue, talking and chatting as new friends will do.

On the outskirts of town they decide to stop
at the local cycling store known as Axel's Bike Shop.
Axel van Springel greets the pair with a welcome ;
he's a gentle old man from a land called Belgium.

Axel is quick to dispense with a treat;
a nice healthy snack keeps the two on their feet.
Van Springel, it seems, is an old cycling great.
He's won races in places quite far from this state.

Lucille and Mike give a "Thanks" and "Goodbye"
and resume their adventure with the sun climbing high.
And speaking of climbing, they head for the hills

where the forces of gravity will soon test their wills.
On the beautiful climbs with the valleys below
you can breathe in the air, you can let your mind go.

Mike dreams of riding to deep outer space, where the planet of Saturn is hosting a race.

The rings around Saturn provide quite a course, as Mike sprints for glory on his outer space horse.

Mike's favorite terrain is the mountainous slopes

of the hills near his home, and he certainly hopes

to be first to the top, no he cannot conceal —

he expects to be quicker than our girl Lucille.

See, some rides are slow and can be quite repetitive

but before you know, things can get quite competitive.

Now wheels are turning and pedals are churning;

their legs and their lungs are feeling the burning!

With sweat on the brow, Mike is wondering how he'll be the first to the top. NO! He can't give up now! Lucille ascends with the greatest of ease climbing high like an acrobat on a trapeze.

The two near the top with an effort so frightful they both crave the victory — it would be so delightful! They twist and contort, they both give it their all but we're sad to report — it's just too... close... to call.

Now they've crested the summit of such a big climb, they've both reached the top in the exact same time.

And with no clear winner on the hill's finish line Lucille and Mike think a tie is just fine.

So they race down the hill with no need to conspire
and at that very moment Mike gets a **FLAT TIRE.**

A hole in one's tire is known as a puncture,
a terrible mishap at any juncture.
But lucky for Mike, he's along with Lucille—
a technician/magician in any ordeal.
As Mike stands aside he can only admire
her skill and her speed with Mike's flattened tire.
So quick as a whistle they're rolling along
with Mike's patched tire feeling steady and strong.

As Mike bids farewell to his new friend Lucille
a realization begins to reveal
that riding alone is a wonderful thing,
but you'll double the fun
with the friends that you bring.

A solo bike ride in the midday sun
is a splendid good time, almost second to none.
But rides are more fun when they include more than one.

FUN

you'll have miles of smiles,
you'll have two tons of fun.

We're so glad you have joined us,
it's so happy we feel,
to see Mike and the Bike
meet Lucille the Wheel!

For more cycling fun,
check out these great websites!

www.Mike and the Bike.com

www.usacycling.org

www.BikesBelong.org

www.saferoutespartnership.org